This Bing book belongs to:

. . . .

Copyright © 2021 Acamar Films Ltd

The *Bing* television series is created by Acamar Films and Brown Bag Films
and adapted from the original books by Ted Dewan.

Bing's Halloween Party is based on the original story *Halloween* written by Susan Earl,
Mikael Shields and Claire Jennings. *Bing's Halloween Party* was first published in Great Britain
by HarperCollins *Children's Books* in 2021 and was adapted from the original story by Rebecca Gerlings.

HarperCollins *Children's Books* is a division of HarperCollins*Publishers* Ltd,
1 London Bridge Street, London SE1 9GF

www.harpercollins.co.uk

HarperCollins*Publishers*
1st Floor, Watermarque Building, Ringsend Road, Dublin 4, Ireland

1 3 5 7 9 10 8 6 4 2

ISBN: 978-0-00-842065-9

Printed in China

MIX
Paper from
responsible sources
FSC® C007454

This book is produced from independently certified FSC™ paper
to ensure responsible forest management.

For more information visit: www.harpercollins.co.uk/green

Bing

Bing's Halloween Party

HarperCollins *Children's Books*

Round the corner, not far away,
Bing is dressing up for Halloween today!

Bing, Sula and Pando are at Amma's, decorating their Halloween costumes. Flop and Amma are carving pumpkins.

"I'm going to do super-bitey teeth now," says Bing.

"RAAAR!"

"And I'm making my wand sparkle!"
says Sula, twirling it in the air.

"Aah harr!" says Pando. "Look at my mango treasure!"

"Oh... yum!" says Sula, looking at the golden fruit inside.

"Biteysaurus is going to eat it all up. **RAAAR!**" says Bing, chasing Pando round the table, giggling.

Amma and Flop come to admire everyone's fancy dress.

"Oh, look at your masks and costumes!" Amma exclaims. "All sparkly... and lots of teeth!"

"We could do with some magic to help us carve these pumpkins," laughs Amma.

Bing and Sula run over to take a look.

"Oh!" gasps Bing. "Are we going to make them all glowy?"

"Yup," replies Flop. "We're going to have glowy pumpkins for our pumpkin party."

Ding-dong!

It's Coco and Charlie! Coco is dressed as an evil queen, and she's turned Charlie into a prickly hedgehog!

"What a **sparkly, bitey, queenly, piratey, prickly** lot we are!" says Amma.

"Look!" says Coco, holding up a cage.
"I've captured my Rainbow Fairy Mice."

"Oh no!" gasps Sula, waving her
magic wand. "I'll rescue them!"

Bing runs to get his Biteysaurus mask,
so he can join in too.

"RAAAR!" he roars, chasing his
friends around the room again.
"Biteysaurus will
capture you!"

But Charlie is scared and starts to cry.

Coco and Sula stop running to find out what's wrong.

"Charlie doesn't like Biteysaurus,
Bing," warns Coco.

"Oh, but Biteysaurus is *me,* Charlie!" says Bing,
opening his mask. "Look! BOO!"

"BING!" says Coco. "Charlie doesn't like it!"

"What's the matter with our little hedgehog?"
asks Amma as she comes over.

"He doesn't
like Bing
RARR-ing,"
Coco explains.

Bing feels sad.
He didn't mean
to upset Charlie.

Bing sits in
a little corner
by the stairs.

"I wonder," says Flop,
coming to find him,
"if there's a Bing
inside this Biteysaurus?"

"Yes," nods Bing, taking off his mask, "but I don't want to go to the pumpkin party any more."

"Why's that, Bing?" asks Flop.

"Um . . ." says Bing, "because Charlie doesn't like me!"

"Why would you think that, Bing?" asks Flop.

"Because when I showed him it was me inside the mask, he didn't like me!" says Bing.

"Ohh," replies Flop. "Do you think Charlie was crying because he thought Biteysaurus had eaten you up?"

"But Biteysaurus isn't real!" replies Bing.

"Hmm," says Flop. "And do you think Charlie *knows* that Biteysaurus isn't real, Bing?"

"Um . . . Ah! Charlie thinks Biteysaurus bited me up!" realises Bing. "Charlie was scared!"

Bing decides to show Charlie that he hasn't been eaten by Biteysaurus.

He kneels down in front of Charlie's buggy to make sure he can see him *without* his mask on first.

"Charlie!" says Bing gently, as he puts on his mask.

"*BOO!*"

This time Charlie giggles,
and feeds Bing some of the mango treasure!
"He likes it, Flop!" exclaims Bing.

"Yum!"

"He certainly does," replies Flop.

"Now, who's ready for our pumpkin party?" asks Amma.

"Me! Me!"
everyone shouts,
rushing over
to admire the
row of beautiful
glowy pumpkins.

Biteysaurus can't wait to get there!

"RAAAR!" he roars excitedly.

When they arrive, they see that the bandstand is surrounded by all the candlelit pumpkins. What a beautiful **pumpkin party!**

Halloween . . . it's a Bing thing!